P9-APP-015

Healthy HABITS™

Blood Pressure Basics

Laura La Bella

rosen publishing's
rosen central®

New York

For my Mom, who has always believed in me

Published in 2011 by The Rosen Publishing Group, Inc.
29 East 21st Street, New York, NY 10010

Library of Congress Cataloging-in-Publication Data

La Bella, Laura.
Blood pressure basics / Laura La Bella.—1st ed.
    p. cm.—(Healthy habits)
Includes bibliographical references and index.
ISBN 978-1-4358-9441-9 (library binding)
ISBN 978-1-4488-0611-9 (pbk. book)
ISBN 978-1-4488-0614-0 (6-pack)
1. Hypertension—Prevention—Juvenile literature. 2. Blood pressure—Juvenile literature. I. Title.
RC685.H8L2 2011
616.1'32—dc22

2009054124

Manufactured in Malaysia

CPSIA Compliance Information: Batch #S10YA: For further information, contact Rosen Publishing, New York, New York, at 1-800-237-9932.

CONTENTS

Introduction

Imagine that the body's arteries are like garden hoses. These tiny pipes carry blood from the heart to the rest of the body. As blood flows through the arteries, it delivers all the necessary oxygen and nutrients the body needs to be healthy. Blood pressure is the force that is applied on the walls of the arteries as blood is pumped to circulate throughout the body. In a garden hose, without some type of pressure, the water can't get from one end to the other. The same is true of the arteries. Without some type of force, the blood cannot circulate throughout the body.

Having blood pressure that is too high or too low can lead to serious medical conditions. High blood pressure can cause a stroke, heart attack, or kidney failure. Low blood pressure can lead to dizziness and fainting. It can also result in a lack of oxygen to the major organs, which can cause them to function improperly.

High blood pressure is the most common chronic illness Americans face. It's estimated that more than sixty-five million people in the United States suffer from high blood pressure, and nearly two million more cases are diagnosed each year. Many people don't even realize they have high blood pressure. The disease may have no symptoms until it has progressed to a later stage that affects the body's organs, like the heart, lungs, or kidneys.

There is good news, though: High blood pressure is controllable and often preventable. It's also relatively easy to detect. Maintaining a healthy blood pressure is important and relatively simple. By visiting the doctor regularly, people can monitor their

A doctor listens to a patient's heart during a routine exam. Getting regular checkups can aid in the early detection of medical conditions, such as high blood pressure.

blood pressure and catch when their blood pressure is too high or too low. There are also things you can do at home to help keep your blood pressure within a healthy range. Eating a diet rich in fruits, vegetables, low-fat dairy, and low-fat meats like chicken and turkey can help greatly in keeping blood pressure in check. Getting regular exercise is also crucial. Exercise helps keep the heart strong and the muscles healthy, and it aids in keeping you at a healthy weight. A healthy weight, a strong heart, and good general health are all good for your blood pressure.

You can live a long life if you have problems with blood pressure, but you must be willing to take special care of yourself and make healthful decisions that will keep your blood pressure under control. You must make good choices about diet and exercise, as well as follow any other suggestions from doctors about ways to stay healthy.

By learning how blood pressure works and by taking care of yourself now, you can help avoid health problems in the future that are associated with changes in blood pressure.

Chapter 1

Blood Pressure Basics

It's not very hard to understand how blood pressure works. All of the organs in the human body need oxygen to survive. Blood carries oxygen and nutrients to the organs through a complex system of blood vessels that reach every single part of the human body, from the fingertips to the heart, lungs, and brain. Each time the heart beats, this system, called the circulatory system, pushes blood through the body, delivering blood, oxygen, and nutrients and removing wastes. As blood travels through the body, it places pressure on the walls of the blood vessels. Blood pressure keeps blood flowing smoothly throughout the body.

There are three main parts—the heart, the arteries, and the kidneys—that affect blood pressure. Arteries are blood vessels that carry oxygen-rich blood away from the heart. The heart pushes blood into the arteries with a certain amount of force. The harder the heart works to push the blood, the greater the force is on the arteries. To accommodate the surge of blood coming from the heart, the arteries contain a layer of muscle that allows them to expand or contract as blood travels through them. When arteries are no longer flexible enough to handle the different levels of blood flow, they can become narrower, making it harder for blood to circulate through them.

The kidneys are important because they help monitor the amount of sodium and the volume of water circulating in the body. The more

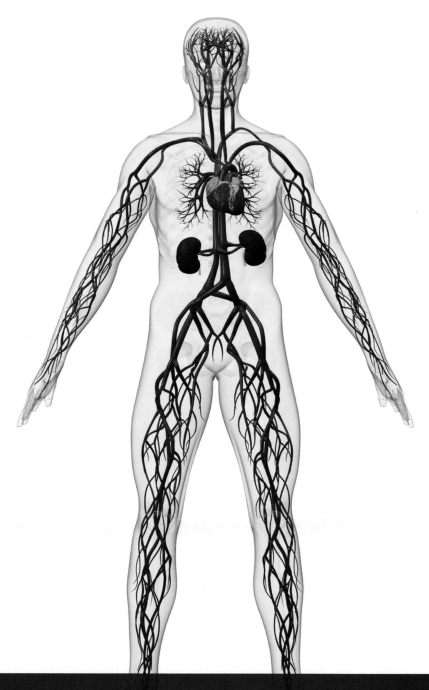

Made up of the heart, blood, and blood vessels, the cardiovascular system distributes oxygen-rich blood throughout the body.

sodium there is in the body, the more water there is in the blood. In a healthy person, when there is a higher intake of salt, the body adjusts. The kidneys excrete (eliminate) more sodium and water, decreasing the pressure on the walls of the arteries. However, if the kidneys are not able to effectively get rid of the excess salt and water, there is an increase in blood volume. This leads to high blood pressure.

Measuring Blood Pressure

Blood pressure is one of the main vital signs, or measurements of body functions, doctors and nurses use to determine general health.

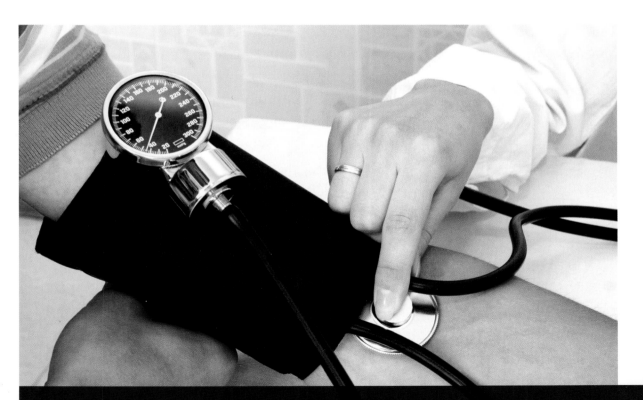

A sphygmomanometer with a fabric cuff is used to measure blood pressure. Regular readings are important for detecting changes in your blood pressure, which can indicate a health problem.

Monitoring blood pressure is important. Changes in blood pressure—whether it's a big rise or a big drop—can be the first sign that you are at risk for health problems now or in the future.

Blood pressure is usually measured by placing a blood pressure cuff around the upper arm, inflating the cuff with air, and listening for changes in the flow of blood. The cuff is part of an instrument called a sphygmomanometer. The sphygmomanometer measures two different forces and gives doctors two different numbers. These numbers are both part of the blood pressure reading. When combined, they tell doctors and nurses what the blood pressure is. A normal blood pressure reading is 120/80. The upper number, called systolic pressure, is the force that occurs as the heart contracts, or squeezes, to pump the blood. The lower number, called diastolic pressure, is the pressure that is reached when the heart rests between beats.

Blood pressure is influenced by the heart rate, the amount of blood pumped by the heart, and the ease with which blood travels through the body. The heart rate is how fast the heart beats. This is measured by the number of times the heart beats in one minute. When the heart rate rises, or the heart beats faster, blood pressure can rise. If the heart beats slowly, blood pressure can drop.

The amount of blood pumped out of the heart with one "squeeze," also called stroke volume, can impact blood pressure. When the body is at rest, the stroke volume is about the same as the amount of blood that the veins carry back to the heart. But under stressful conditions, the nervous system can increase stroke volume by making the heart pump harder. This puts stress on the walls of the arteries.

Another important element that affects blood pressure is how well blood travels through the veins and arteries. If a person has blockage or narrowing caused by clogged arteries, the blood may have difficulty traveling through the body due to increased resistance in the blood vessels. The heart must then pump harder to push the blood through these clogged areas.

Even in children, blood pressure should be checked occasionally, beginning at about age two. After age twenty-one, blood pressure needs to be checked at least once every two years. Often, when you visit the doctor for a checkup, or if you have a cold or the flu, he or she will take your blood pressure as part of the examination.

What Is High Blood Pressure?

Normal blood pressure fluctuates. At certain times, it might go up; sometimes, it will remain steady. This is very normal. For example, if someone witnesses a car crash or is excessively nervous before a big test or game, blood pressure may rise. Blood pressure also rises during exercise. These are all normal occurrences, and blood pressure soon returns to normal.

When one's blood pressure is high all the time, though, it means there is a consistent increased force on the blood vessel walls. This can lead to damage to both blood vessels and organs, which can result in serious illness. High blood pressure is a significant health problem in the United States. More than sixty-five million Americans suffer from high blood pressure and/or from problems related to the condition. That's about 25 percent of the country's adult population.

The medical term for high blood pressure is hypertension. This doesn't mean that people get high blood pressure from being tense or nervous. Even calm, relaxed people can have high blood pressure.

There are three different kinds of hypertension. Primary hypertension is the most common type of high blood pressure. Doctors suspect that a combination of lifestyle, diet, heredity, age, gender, race/ethnicity, and other factors contribute to this type of high blood pressure. Secondary hypertension is high blood pressure that has a definite cause, which may be temporary or controllable. People might

Excessive stress, as well as a poor diet, lack of exercise, and being overweight, can lead to high blood pressure.

have secondary hypertension as a result of hormonal problems, kidney disease, or head injuries. The third type of high blood pressure is isolated systolic hypertension. This is a type of blood pressure that mainly affects older people. In this condition, a person's blood pressure is higher than normal when the heart beats but then returns to normal between heartbeats. This kind of hypertension is usually due to the hardening of the blood vessels, which commonly occurs as people age.

What Causes High Blood Pressure?

The exact causes of high blood pressure are not well known, but there are a number of factors that play a role in a person developing the condition:

- Smoking tobacco
- Being overweight
- Lack of physical activity
- Too much salt in the diet
- Stress
- Aging
- Genetics
- Family history of high blood pressure
- Medical conditions (such as chronic kidney disease or hormone disorders)

Some of these factors are easy to control. People can control how much salt they eat. If they

Who Is Most Likely to Develop High Blood Pressure?

Some people are more likely to develop high blood pressure than others. There are several factors that can make a person more likely to develop high blood pressure, among them:

- Having family members with high blood pressure
- Smoking
- African American heritage
- Pregnancy
- Being over the age of thirty-five
- Being overweight or obese
- Leading a sedentary lifestyle, or being inactive
- Drinking a lot of alcohol
- Being under a lot of stress

are overweight, eating a healthy diet and exercising can help them lose weight and lower blood pressure. However, there are other factors that people cannot control. These include a family history of high blood pressure, race/ethnicity, and genetics. These factors aren't changeable, but that doesn't mean a person is destined to have high blood pressure if a parent or grandparent has it.

High blood pressure initially has no symptoms. It may be impossible to detect unless you visit a doctor on a regular basis. In fact, many people have high blood pressure for years without knowing it. If left untreated, high blood pressure can lead to damaged blood

Healthful eating is important. A diet rich in fresh fruits, vegetables, whole grains, and lean meats helps you maintain a healthy weight and a healthy blood pressure.

vessels, heart disease, congestive heart failure, stroke, and damage to other vital organs. It can also affect eyesight.

High blood pressure can be treated in a number of ways. A critical step in preventing and treating high blood pressure is adopting a healthful lifestyle. Patients can lower their blood pressure by getting more exercise and eating a healthful diet rich in fruits and vegetables. Avoiding salt is another key to treating high blood pressure. Doctors may also prescribe medication that can help treat high blood pressure.

What Is Low Blood Pressure?

Low blood pressure, also called hypotension, is when blood pressure drops below about 90/60. In healthy, fit people, low blood pressure is a sign of good cardiovascular (heart and blood vessel) health. For those who are not healthy or physically fit, low blood pressure can lead to dizziness and fainting. It can be a sign that an underlying problem is causing poor blood flow to the heart, brain, and other vital organs. This is especially true in older people.

A person with low blood pressure may experience symptoms from the lack of blood flowing through the arteries and veins. When the flow of blood is too low, vital organs, such as the brain, heart, and kidneys, don't get enough oxygen and nutrients to function properly. For example, if the brain does not get enough blood and brain cells do not receive enough oxygen and nutrients, a person can feel light-headed or dizzy. Sometimes a person can even faint. Without sufficient blood flow, our kidneys can fail to rid waste from our bodies, chest pain can develop from a lack of oxygen to our hearts, and our livers and lungs can begin to have trouble functioning.

Abnormally low blood pressure, or hypotension, is a serious illness. It can lead to dizziness and fainting, and it can affect how well one's vital organs function.

Treating High and Low Blood Pressure

There are a number of ways to treat high and low blood pressure. Sometimes doctors recommend medication that can help lower high blood pressure. For example, there are medications that help the kidneys flush excess water and sodium from the body. Some medications cause the heart to beat more slowly so that it exerts less force on the arteries. Others help the arteries to relax and widen to allow increased blood flow.

Diet and exercise can have a big impact on high blood pressure, too. In some people, eating healthfully and getting enough exercise can produce the same results as medication. Not only do diet and exercise help lower high blood pressure, but they also improve over-all health. These healthy habits enable people to fight off illness more easily and possibly avoid other medical conditions.

Low blood pressure may be treated in a number of ways. Depending on one's age, health status, and the type of low blood pressure an individual has, he or she has a number of options for treating it:

- **Use more salt.** Experts usually recommend limiting the amount of salt in your diet because sodium can raise blood pressure, sometimes dramatically. For people with low blood pressure, that can be a good thing. Because excess sodium can lead to heart failure, especially in older adults, it's important to check with a doctor before increasing salt in the diet.

- **Drink more water.** Although nearly everyone can benefit from drinking more water, this is especially true for people with low blood pressure. Fluids increase blood volume and help prevent dehydration. Both are important in treating hypotension.

- **Medication.** Several medications, either used alone or together, may be suggested by a doctor to treat low blood pressure. For example, some drugs boost blood volume, which raises blood pressure. Doctors can prescribe the correct drug, or combination of drugs, to treat each patient and his or her particular situation most effectively.

Ten Great Questions
to Ask a Doctor

1. What causes high or low blood pressure?

2. What is normal blood pressure?

3. What can I do to help improve my blood pressure?

4. How do I know if I have high or low blood pressure?

5. What health problems are associated with high and low blood pressure?

6. What treatments are available if I have a problem with my blood pressure?

7. How can I avoid problems with my blood pressure?

8. If my parents have problems with their blood pressure, does that mean I will, too?

9. How can diet and exercise help keep me healthy?

10. Where can I go to exercise if I can't afford a gym membership?

Chapter 2

Changing One's Diet

A healthy diet can be very helpful for keeping blood pressure within a normal range. Doctors often recommend a diet that includes a lot of fruits and vegetables and is low in salt. Other healthful diet changes include eating low-fat dairy; avoiding foods that are high in saturated fat and cholesterol; eating more whole grains, fish, and poultry; and eating foods rich in magnesium, potassium, and calcium.

Eating a healthy diet is important because high blood pressure is more common in people who are overweight. One can maintain a healthy weight by eating properly and getting enough exercise. High blood pressure is one of the leading causes of preventable illnesses and death in the United States. By changing what they eat, people can have a big impact on their overall health, as well as avoid the many health problems associated with high blood pressure.

What Is Sodium?

Avoiding salt is a key diet change doctors recommend to patients who are dealing with high blood pressure. Salt, also called sodium, is a mineral composed primarily of sodium chloride. While it is essential for life, too much of it can be hazardous.

Salt is an important preservative and a popular food seasoning. It is also one of the primary electrolytes found in the body. Electrolytes

Blood pressure problems are among the most preventable illnesses, and a healthy diet is key. Eating meals that include lean protein and vegetables can have a great impact on your health.

are important because they are essential for the normal functioning of cells, tissues, and organs. Common electrolytes include sodium, potassium, chloride, and bicarbonate. Sodium is essential in small amounts. It helps maintain the balance of fluids in the body, helps transmit nerve impulses, and influences the contraction and relaxation of muscles. The kidneys regulate the amount of sodium kept in the body. When sodium levels are low, the kidneys conserve sodium. When sodium levels are high, the kidneys excrete the excess amount.

Sodium can negatively affect blood pressure, causing it to rise due to increased water retention in the blood vessels. Sodium impacts blood pressure when the kidneys fail to get rid of the extra sodium in a person's diet. The Dietary Guidelines for Americans jointly issued by the U.S. Department of Health and Human Services and the U.S. Department of Agriculture recommend that people take in no more than 2,300 milligrams of sodium each day.

Frozen dinners and fast food fit in well with our busy schedules. However, these processed food choices are often high in salt, which can lead to high blood pressure.

According to the Mayo Clinic, about 11 percent of the sodium found in the average U.S. diet comes from adding salt or other sodium-rich condiments (ketchup, mustard, soy sauce) to foods while cooking or eating. However, the vast majority of the sodium Americans consume—a whopping 77 percent—comes from eating prepared or processed foods. Processed foods are any item that has been boxed, bagged, canned, or jarred. This includes boxed creamy macaroni and rice dishes, junk food like potato chips and dips, frozen foods like pizza and TV dinners, pickles, and even candy bars. Salt is found in nearly all processed foods and is one of the ways companies preserve foods to keep them from spoiling. Salt is also used to enhance flavor. It makes soups more savory, reduces dryness in crackers and pretzels, and even increases sweetness in cakes and cookies. Canned and frozen foods are often especially high in sodium.

The term "processed food" also includes fast-food burgers, greasy French fries, fried chicken and chicken nuggets, and soda—all the items sold at fast-food restaurant chains. Fast food is among the worst processed food you can eat. Aside from it being high in calories and fat, fast food is also full of sodium. A typical fast-food hamburger has about 1,000 mg of sodium. If a customer eats a full fast-food meal, which includes a sandwich, a medium-sized serving of French fries, and a medium soft drink, the sodium for the entire meal is about 1,300 mg, which is more than half of the daily recommended intake of sodium.

Because we have become a nation that is busy and eats on the go, the average American now consumes more than 3,400 mg of sodium per day. In moderation and as part of an overall healthful diet, eating a small amount of processed food is OK. A few potato chips

Ways to Reduce Sodium in the Diet

There are a lot of foods that are high in sodium, even some unexpected ones, like soda and pizza, or mustard and cheese. By choosing the right foods, it is easy to reduce the amount of sodium consumed in the daily diet. Just follow the guidelines below:

- Choose fresh, frozen, or canned food items without added salt.
- Select unsalted nuts or seeds, dried beans, peas, and lentils.
- Limit the number of salty snacks you eat, like potato chips and pretzels.
- Avoid adding salt and canned vegetables to homemade dishes.
- Select unsalted, fat-free broths or soups.
- Select fat-free or low-fat milk, low-sodium and low-fat cheeses, as well as low-fat yogurt.
- When dining out at a restaurant, ask for the food to be prepared without salt.
- Use spices and herbs to enhance the taste of the food instead of salt.

or some candy once in a while is fine. When the majority of someone's diet is made up of these food items, though, he or she isn't getting the right mix of nutrients, vitamins, and minerals the body needs to remain healthy. The individual is also eating more sodium than he or she needs, which over time can harm the kidneys and raise blood pressure.

Being aware of sodium and how it's used in food preparation is half the battle in eating less of it. To understand how much sodium is in food, check the labels found on the back of food products and the

Instead of eating out or purchasing unhealthy fast food, opt for healthy snacks, like fresh fruit. Fruit is low in calories, high in vitamins and minerals, and naturally sweet.

nutritional information on restaurant Web sites. Both will display how much sodium is in the food you commonly purchase in stores or eat in restaurants. Some of the most common foods that are high in sodium are convenience foods, salad dressings, and condiments, like mustard and ketchup. Reading labels at the grocery store can be helpful in identifying which foods are high in sodium. Just look on the label for "sodium" and read the amount next to it. The label will show how much sodium is in each serving of that particular food. Knowing how to order at a restaurant can also help. Most chefs will leave out salt upon request.

Eating a Healthy Diet

Research has shown that eating a healthy diet can reduce the risk of developing high blood pressure. It can also help lower high blood pressure for patients who have already been diagnosed with the condition. A healthy diet that focuses on fruits, vegetables, and low-fat dairy products is best. It is also wise to avoid foods high in saturated fat, total fat, and cholesterol. Eating less fat is very important. Evidence shows that a low-fat diet may decrease cholesterol and the risk for coronary artery disease. Cholesterol is found in every cell in the human body and is used to build healthy cells. When you have high cholesterol, you may develop fatty deposits in the blood vessels. Eventually, these deposits make it difficult for enough blood to flow through the arteries. Eating a high-fat diet increases the risk for these fatty deposits. A low-fat diet helps prevent clogged arteries.

Potassium in moderation may improve blood pressure. Potassium is an electrolyte that also helps the kidneys function normally.

The best diet is one full of fruits and vegetables, whole grains, poultry, fish, and nuts, but with reduced amounts of fat, red meat, sweets, and sugared beverages. Categories of healthful foods include:

- **Grains:** Whole grains, which contain all edible parts of the grain, include whole-grain corn, oats, popcorn, brown rice, whole rye, and whole-grain barley. The fiber and nutrients in whole grains may help prevent high blood pressure.
- **Vegetables:** They contain many kinds of healthful nutrients, vitamins, and minerals that help keep a person healthy. Eating a wide variety of vegetables, from dark leafy greens to bright red peppers and colorful yellow squash, can give an individual practically all the nutrients his or her body needs to be healthy. Vegetables are also very low in calories and contain almost no fat.
- **Fruits:** Packed with essential nutrients, vitamins, and anti-oxidants, fruit is an easy way to add a taste of something sweet to a daily diet without an excess of sugar and calories. Fruit is full of fiber, and some varieties, such as bananas, are high in potassium, which can help lower high blood pressure.
- **Low-fat or fat-free dairy products:** Eating low-fat dairy products is proven to aid in weight loss and in lowering blood pressure.
- **Lean meat, poultry, and fish:** Red meat can cause an increase in blood cholesterol, which can lead to increased blood pressure. Those who eat lean meats, poultry, and fish tend to have lower cholesterol, which makes these sources of protein healthier choices.

- **Nuts, seeds, and legumes:** Perfect snack choices, nuts and seeds are a great source of protein and healthful fat. The protein in nuts is much better for you than the protein found in red meat, which can increase the levels of cholesterol in the blood.

As we have discussed, avoiding processed foods is also important. These foods, which include canned foods, frozen dinners, and prepared foods, often use large amounts of salt for flavor and as a preservative. The biggest blood pressure–lowering benefits come from diets that have low levels of sodium (around 1,500 mg) per day.

MYTHS and FACTS

Only people with hyper personalities and people who are tense and nervous suffer from high blood pressure.

Anyone can get high blood pressure; being nervous or agitated doesn't necessarily lead to the condition. However, learning to reduce stress and deal with negative emotions can help keep you healthier.

Changing one's diet will not help lower blood pressure.

The right diet not only can reduce blood pressure, it can also lower one's risk of other health conditions, such as diabetes, heart attack, cancer, and stroke. Many doctors suggest adopting a healthy diet as a way to treat high blood pressure successfully.

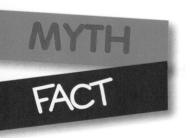

You can't die from high blood pressure.

Every two minutes, a person in the United States dies from a health complication related to high blood pressure. Uncontrolled high blood pressure can lead to heart attack, heart failure, stroke, and kidney failure. High blood pressure itself may not directly lead to death, but the damage it can cause to the body can.

Chapter 3

How Exercise Can Help

By now, most people know that exercise is a healthy habit. You have most likely heard a physical education teacher or sports coach talk about ways to become stronger, faster, or healthier by participating in sports or other physical activities.

Exercise is more than just fun and games. Yes, being physically fit can help one perform better in sports, whether you are a serious athlete or enjoy playing dodgeball with friends. Exercise can also help prevent chronic health conditions, strengthen the heart and muscles, promote weight loss, and improve the quality of sleep. It's possible to gain the health benefits of exercise by walking as little as ten to fifteen minutes per day.

By understanding the benefits of exercise now, at a young age, it's possible to lead a healthy lifestyle that will last well into adulthood. It's easy to find activities to enjoy and participate in throughout life, like dancing, running, or golf. It's important to learn how to take care of yourself through exercise, how exercise can impact blood pressure, and the types of exercise that can produce the biggest benefits.

How Are Exercise and Blood Pressure Related?

It may not be obvious, but regular physical activity is essential for leading a healthy life. It makes the heart stronger, and it helps blood

Exercise is a vital component of leading a healthy lifestyle. It helps build muscle and bone, and it strengthens the heart. Exercise also reduces stress, lifts mood, and improves sleep.

move through the body more efficiently. Each time someone goes for a walk or run, takes a spinning class, or lifts weights, he or she is making the heart and muscles stronger. A strong heart can pump more blood through the body with less effort. If the heart works less, the force on the arteries decreases, which lowers blood pressure.

Obesity, or being overweight, is one of the strongest risk factors for developing high blood pressure. About one in three American adults is considered to be obese. Being overweight is quickly becoming an increasing health problem not only in the United States, but all around the world. Being overweight means being at a higher risk for cancer, depression, heart disease, skin problems, sleep disorders, stroke, diabetes, and high blood pressure. Being overweight makes treating high blood pressure much more difficult.

Even small changes in one's weight and fitness can have a big impact on health. Studies have proven that losing even 5 to 10 pounds (2 to 4 kilograms) has positive benefits for lowering blood pressure. Becoming more physically active lowers the systolic blood pressure (the top number in a blood pressure reading) by an average of 5 to 10 millimeters. That's as good as some blood pressure medications. And as an added benefit, exercise has beneficial side effects, unlike those that come from taking medication. The side effects of exercise include not only losing weight, but also sleeping better, gaining muscle strength, strengthening the heart, improving mood, and boosting energy level. For some people, getting exercise each day is enough to reduce the need for blood pressure medication. Exercise also helps people maintain steady blood pressure. If blood pressure is at a desirable level, in the range of 120/80 or lower, exercise can keep blood pressure from rising as people get older. To keep blood pressure low, it is necessary to keep exercising. It takes about one to

Even small changes can have a big impact on our health. Losing just 5 to 10 pounds (2 to 4 kilograms) can have positive benefits for one's blood pressure.

three months for regular exercise to have an impact on blood pressure, but the benefits last only as long as exercise is continued.

Types of Exercise

With all of the different ways to get exercise, from aerobic classes like spinning and kickboxing to weight training, running, and swimming, which kind makes the biggest difference? Weight training increases flexibility and strength, but to really have an impact on blood pressure

Cardiovascular exercise—such as running, aerobics, biking, swimming, and soccer—boosts the heart rate and improves endurance.

it's necessary to burn calories through aerobic exercise. Regular aerobic exercise can prevent and reduce high blood pressure.

Aerobic exercise is any physical activity that increases the heart and breathing rates. Aerobic exercises include walking, jogging, jumping rope, bicycling (indoor or outdoor), playing tag, cross-country skiing, skating, rowing, high-impact or low-impact aerobics,

Starting a Fitness Program

Starting a fitness program may be one of the best things to do for health. And it's easy. Just follow these steps:

Step 1: Assess fitness level.

Most people have some idea of how fit they are. Assessing and recording some basic fitness scores can provide a starting point and a way to measure progress. Consider recording one or more of the following:

- Your pulse rate before and after a 1-mile (1.6 kilometers) walk
- How long it takes to walk 1 mile (1.6 kilometers)
- How many push-ups you can do in thirty seconds
- How far you can reach forward while seated on the floor with the legs straight out in front of you

Step 2: Create a fitness program.

It's easy to say that you'll exercise every day, but to know what you'll do each day requires a plan. Decide what the goals are. To run faster, consider a plan that focuses on running and increasing speed. Do you want to be able to play a full game of soccer and not be so tired? To accomplish this, you need to build endurance with aerobic exercise.

Step 3: What equipment do I need to get started?

You'll probably need the basics, which is a good pair of athletic shoes. Be sure to pick shoes designed for the activity you will participate in because running and cross-training shoes are much different than walking shoes. What about other equipment? Do you need weights, a swimsuit for laps in the pool, or a bike for cycling outdoors? No matter what you need, make sure you buy equipment that is enjoyable and easy to use so that you will continue with the exercise plan.

Step 4: Get started.

Now you're ready for action. Start slowly and build up gradually. If you try to run a mile today without having ever run before, you'll just end up in pain and possibly injured. Start small and be consistent to see all the benefits. Try different activities to keep from getting bored and, most important, listen to your body. If you start to feel dizzy or you feel pain, take a break or stop.

swimming, and water aerobics. Most sports like soccer, basketball, baseball, track, lacrosse, and football fall into this category. It also includes activities like mowing the lawn, raking leaves, or doing housework, such as vacuuming and scrubbing the floor. Basically, if the activity takes effort and one's heart rate increases as a result of the activity, it is aerobic exercise.

To get the maximum benefits of exercise, experts recommend gradually working up to doing an aerobic activity that lasts for twenty to thirty minutes at least three to four times a week. This amount of exercise will have an impact on weight loss, will strengthen the heart, and will increase muscle conditioning. Exercising at least every other day helps one maintain a regular exercise schedule and allows the body to rest between workouts.

Reasons to Exercise

Aside from exercise being part of a healthy lifestyle, it can have a positive impact on many areas of life. There are many reasons to exercise. Exercise can help one do the following:

1. **Maintain a healthy weight.** Combined with a healthy diet, aerobic exercise helps in losing weight—and keeping it off.
2. **Increase stamina.** Aerobic exercise may make you tired in the

Exercise can be a fun group activity, too. You can meet new friends and enjoy yourself while learning how to live a healthy lifestyle.

short term. Over the long term, one can enjoy increased stamina and reduced fatigue. In other words, it will be possible to engage in activities for longer periods of time without becoming tired or short of breath.

3. **Avoid illness.** Aerobic exercise activates the immune system. This leaves you less susceptible to minor viral illnesses, such as colds and flu. It also helps you recover faster when you do get sick.

4. **Reduce health risks.** Aerobic exercise reduces the risk of many conditions, including obesity, heart disease, high blood pressure, type 2 diabetes, stroke, and certain types of cancer. Weight-bearing aerobic exercises, such as walking, that require you to use your own weight as resistance reduce one's risk for diseases like osteoporosis.

5. **Manage chronic conditions.** Aerobic exercise helps lower high blood pressure and control blood sugar. It can also help people manage conditions that have already been diagnosed. For example, patients who have had heart attacks often turn to exercise because it can help prevent another attack from occurring.

6. **Strengthen the heart.** If you have a strong heart, it doesn't need to beat as fast and it can pump blood more efficiently. A strong heart also helps improve blood flow to all parts of the body.

7. **Keep the arteries clear.** Aerobic exercise helps keep cholesterol in check. There are two kinds of cholesterol, good cholesterol and bad cholesterol. Good cholesterol, also called high-density lipoprotein or HDL, removes excess cholesterol from the arteries. Bad cholesterol, also called

Tips to Get You Moving

Don't be afraid to get active.
Start slowly with something you enjoy, like taking walks or riding a bicycle around the neighborhood.

Find something you like.
If you love the outdoors, combine being outside with exercise. Go hiking, kayaking, or jogging to enjoy the outdoors. Learn a new sport.

Mix up activities.
A variety of activities helps you stay interested in exercise and keeps you motivated. Running every day might lead to boredom after a while, so mix it up by adding a day or two of swimming. Get some friends together to play baseball or basketball at a local park or community center.

Invite friends and make it social.
Ask friends if they might be interested in joining you for a workout. There are a lot of activities that you can do as a group, like walking, running, or playing soccer. You can even create fitness challenges, like an obstacle course, to make it more fun and competitive.

Celebrate accomplishments.
Finding ways to celebrate success is important. Keep a log to mark the distances you reached when running or how often you exercised. Give yourself a treat when you've reached a goal, such as running a mile or doing ten push-ups. Don't forget to keep challenging yourself!

low-density lipoprotein or LDL, causes buildup in the arteries and can create blockages. Exercise helps keep the arteries clear and healthy.

8. **Boost the mood.** Aerobic exercise can ease depression, reduce the tension associated with anxiety, and promote relaxation. When we exercise, we release endorphins, substances found in the brain that lead to a feeling of happiness and well-being.

9. **Stay active and independent as you get older.** Aerobic exercise keeps the muscles strong, which can help you maintain mobility as you get older. Aerobic exercise also keeps the mind sharp. At least thirty minutes of aerobic exercise three days a week seems to reduce cognitive (mental) decline in older adults.

10. **Live longer.** People who participate in regular aerobic exercise appear to live longer than those who don't exercise regularly. This is mainly due to having a stronger heart, better muscle conditioning, better quality of sleep, and a healthier lifestyle overall.

Chapter 4

Other Healthy Habits

About one in every four American adults has high blood pressure. It's an especially dangerous disease because it often has no warning signs or symptoms. Fortunately, it's easy to detect blood pressure problems by having your blood pressure checked regularly. If you have consistently high or low readings, you can take the necessary steps (diet changes, exercise, etc.) to get it under control. If you have normal blood pressure, you can learn how to keep it steady. The goal is to avoid the health problems that arise from having high or low blood pressure. The first line of defense against high blood pressure, before or after the condition is diagnosed, is making lifestyle changes that can positively affect health.

Establish Healthy Habits Now

Practicing healthy habits now can delay the onset of high blood pressure or greatly reduce the odds that you will develop high blood pressure. While you cannot control genetics or family history, you can have a big impact on blood pressure by maintaining a healthy diet and incorporating regular exercise into your lifestyle. These choices play a big role in overall health, helping one maintain a healthy cardio-vascular system and avoid additional health problems.

Healthy Habits That Improve Quality of Life

There are many easy ways to boost the chances of living a healthy life now and in the future. By making some changes now and becoming more aware of what behaviors are healthy, you can ensure that you will have a healthy adulthood and live a long life.

Healthy Habit 1: Eat Breakfast

Research shows that people who eat breakfast tend to take in more vitamins and minerals. They also tend to eat less during the day and make healthier food choices. A 2003 American Heart Association report also supports eating breakfast. It states that breakfast eaters are significantly less likely to be obese and develop diabetes compared with non-breakfast eaters.

Healthy Habit 2: Protect the Skin

Our skin starts to age as soon as we are born, and the best way to protect it is to stay out of the sun. If you are outside when it's sunny, be sure to use a sunscreen with an SPF of 15 or higher, wear a hat or other protective clothing, and avoid sunbathing. Sun exposure can damage skin, and that damage shows up as wrinkles or worse. Sun exposure is a leading cause of skin cancer.

Healthy Habit 3: Drink Water

Our bodies need water to stay hydrated. Our vital organs, such as the heart, brain, kidney, and liver, need water to function properly. Drinking water also keeps you from consuming less healthful beverages, like sodas, which are full of sugar and caffeine.

Healthy Habit 4: Eat Dairy

The calcium found in dairy products, like milk, cheese, and yogurt, helps one develop strong bones and teeth. Studies have also shown that dairy can have a positive impact on lowering high blood pressure.

When most people think of healthy habits, they think of brushing their teeth each morning and night, washing their hands to prevent the spread of germs, and eating fruits and vegetables. These are important, but there are additional healthy habits to consider when it comes to keeping one's health in check.

Healthy eating and exercise aren't the only good habits you should be developing that will have an impact on blood pressure. You can help control the odds of developing a blood pressure condition by avoiding tobacco products, reducing stress, limiting or avoiding caffeine, and getting enough rest.

Just like brushing your teeth every day and washing your hands to prevent the spread of illnesses, having your blood pressure checked regularly is important for staying healthy.

Say "No" to Tobacco

Nicotine, a chemical found in tobacco products like cigarettes, is a poison that is very dangerous to one's health. In addition to all the information out there about tobacco causing cancer, tobacco products can wreak havoc on the body as a whole.

When you use tobacco products, less oxygen flows in the blood, so major organs don't receive as much as they need. Tobacco products also increase blood pressure and heart rate, cause blood-clotting problems, and damage the blood vessels that help deliver oxygen and nutrients to the organs. Smoking also injures blood vessel walls and speeds up the hardening of the arteries. This means that the blood passing through those arteries has a more difficult time circulating in the body. As a result, the heart must beat harder or faster to push the blood through. This causes blood pressure to rise.

By deciding not to smoke, you can avoid many serious health problems. You will live longer if you don't smoke, and you'll reduce the risk of developing one of several serious diseases. You significantly cut down your risk of developing lung cancer, other lung diseases, and heart diseases, including heart attacks. If you don't smoke, you'll also steer clear of stained teeth and the loss of your senses of smell and taste.

Connected: Stress and Blood Pressure

Stress is often defined as a fight-or-flight response. There are moments when the body produces stress hormones in preparation for fighting stress or running away from it. This type of response was useful for people thousands of years ago when they were faced with

Tobacco products are dangerous to your health, so refusing them is a good idea. They can cause cancer, damage the blood vessels, and lead to heart disease and stroke.

a wild animal or another threat. Today, our bodies continue to respond in a similar way. Instead of running away from a wild animal, we face threats such as speaking in public, being unprepared for a test, or breaking the law.

Stressful situations can cause blood pressure to spike temporarily. Even though many researchers have studied the link between high blood pressure and stress, there's no proof that stress by itself is a cause of high blood pressure. However, doctors do know that high levels of stress can make other conditions, such as high cholesterol, worse. This in turn impacts blood pressure. When you are under stress, you are less likely to eat healthfully, and you may overeat. You also may not get the proper amount of exercise.

When people are exposed to long periods of stress, their bodies give warning signs that something is wrong. These signs of stress—which include constant worry, anxiety, nervousness, compulsive eating, muscle tension, achiness, and grinding the teeth—should not be ignored. They are signs that our bodies are telling us we need to slow down, relax more, and give ourselves a break from stressful situations.

To cope with stress, medical professionals suggest reducing the causes of stress as quickly as possible. You should also make the effort to eat as healthfully as possible, get regular exercise, and get enough rest. These small steps will help you deal with the stressful situation until it can be resolved.

Limit Outside Stimulants

Caffeine is a mild stimulant found in coffee, tea, chocolate, and most soft drinks. Too much caffeine can cause nervousness and the

Eating large amounts of fast food leads to poor health, weight gain, and an increased chance of developing various health problems.

jitters. It may also increase blood pressure. Blood pressure is measured in millimeters of mercury (mmHg). Studies have found that the amount of caffeine in two to three cups of coffee can raise systolic pressure (the top number) by 3 to 14 millimeters and diastolic pressure (the bottom number) by 4 to 13 millimeters in people who do not have a problem with high blood pressure.

What can cause this spike in blood pressure? Some researchers think that caffeine temporarily narrows blood vessels by blocking the effects of a hormone that helps keep blood vessels open.

Coffee and soda aren't the only drinks that have high levels of caffeine. Energy drinks should also be avoided. Energy drinks are often loaded with caffeine, sugar, and herbal stimulants. These can cause a number of health problems, such as restlessness, mood swings, weight gain, and high blood pressure. It's often best to drink plain water during a workout or while practicing for sports.

Rest Up

Recent studies suggest that sleep deprivation may increase the risk of high blood pressure. One study found that regularly sleeping less than seven or eight hours a night puts people at risk for high blood pressure. Not getting enough sleep is proven to affect the body's stress response, which can raise the risks of developing high blood pressure. It has also been linked to weight gain, diabetes, depression, and the overall health of the heart.

Our bodies function differently while we sleep. One of sleep's biggest benefits is that while we are asleep, our heart rate and blood pressure go down. This doesn't happen during quick naps, though. It's only when we sleep for periods of time that are five hours in length

It is important to get enough sleep each night. Sleep helps the body grow and repair itself from damage. Sleep also keeps the mind sharp and helps control weight.

or longer. It has been reported that on average, each hour of missed sleep per night raises the likelihood by 37 percent that a person could develop high blood pressure.

Getting enough sleep needs to become a part of one's healthy lifestyle, in addition to a healthy diet, getting enough exercise, and other healthy habits.

GLOSSARY

aerobic Increasing oxygen consumption for metabolic processes in the body.

antioxidant A substance that prevents reactions with oxygen.

arteries Elastic-walled vessels that carry blood from the heart through the body.

cardiovascular Relating to or involving the heart and blood vessels.

cholesterol A waxy substance found in the body's cells and the blood plasma. High blood cholesterol is a risk factor for heart disease.

circulatory system A network of arteries, veins, and capillaries that transports blood throughout the body.

diabetes A condition in which the body either does not produce enough of, or does not properly respond to, a hormone called insulin.

electrolytes Minerals in the blood that carry an electric charge, needed for the normal functioning of cells and organs.

endorphins Compounds released by the body in response to exercise, pain, or excitement, which produce feelings of well-being.

genetics A branch of biology that deals with heredity.

heart disease An abnormal condition of the heart, or of the heart and blood vessels.

hypertension Abnormally high blood pressure.

hypotension Abnormally low blood pressure.

immune system A system that protects the body against foreign substances, infection, and disease.

nicotine The poisonous chemical found in tobacco products that makes them addictive.

preservative A natural or synthetic chemical that is added to products, such as foods, to keep them from spoiling.

processed foods Foods that have been altered from their natural state for taste, appearance, or convenience. Many processed foods are made with trans fats, saturated fats, artificial flavors and colorings, chemical preservatives, fillers, and sodium.

SPF Sun protection factor; a measurement of the effectiveness of sunscreen to protect the skin from the ultraviolet rays of the sun.

sphygmomanometer An instrument for measuring blood pressure.

stamina The capability of sustaining prolonged stressful effort.

stimulant A chemical that induces temporary improvements in mental or physical function or both.

stroke volume The amount of blood pumped with each beat of the heart.

vital signs Measurements of various physical statistics, often taken by health professionals, in order to assess the most basic body functions.

whole grain Of or being a natural or unprocessed grain, containing the germ and the bran. Whole-grain products include breads, pastas, and cereals that are made with whole-grain flours and not with white, processed flours.

American Heart Association
National Center
7272 Greenville Avenue
Dallas, TX 75231
(800) 242-8721
Web site: http://www.americanheart.org
This nonprofit organization provides information, education, and
     care in an effort to reduce disability and death caused by cardio-
     vascular disease and stroke. It provides a wealth of materials
     and resources to help people achieve a heart-healthy lifestyle.

American Society of Hypertension
148 Madison Avenue, 5th Floor
New York, NY 10016
(212) 696-9099
Web site: http://www.ash-us.org
This U.S. professional organization of scientific investigators and
     health care professionals is committed to eliminating hyperten-
     sion and its consequences.

Canadian Hypertension Society
Secretariat Office
Queen's University
Botterell Hall, 5th Floor
Kingston, ON K7L 3N6
Canada
(613) 533-3299

Web site: http://www.hypertension.ca
This organization promotes the prevention and control of hypertension through research and education.

Heart and Stroke Foundation of Canada
222 Queen Street, Suite 1402
Ottawa, ON K1P 5V9
Canada
(613) 569-4361
Web site: http://www.heartandstroke.com
This volunteer-based health organization works to eliminate heart
disease and stroke. It also seeks to reduce the impact of both
through the advancement of research, the promotion of healthy
living, and advocacy.

International Society on Hypertension in Blacks (ISHIB)
157 Summit View Drive
McDonough, GA 30253
(404) 880-0343
Web site: http://www.ishib.org
The ISHIB's mission is to improve the health and life expectancy of
ethnic minority populations around the world.

National Heart, Blood, and Lung Institute
P.O. Box 30105
Bethesda, MD 20824-0105
(301) 592-8573

Web site: http://www.nhlbi.nih.gov
This institute provides global leadership for research, training, and
education programs in order to promote the prevention and
treatment of heart, lung, and blood diseases. It seeks to enhance
the health of all individuals so that they can live longer and more
fulfilling lives.

Web Sites

Due to the changing nature of Internet links, Rosen Publishing has
developed an online list of Web sites related to the subject of this
book. This site is updated regularly. Please use this link to access
the list:

http://www.rosenlinks.com/hab/bloo

FOR FURTHER READING

Anspaugh, David J., and Gene Ezell. *Teaching Today's Health*. San Francisco, CA: Benjamin Cummings, 2009.

Bakewell, Lisa. *Fitness Information for Teens: Health Tips About Exercise, Physical Well-Being, and Health Maintenance*. Detroit, MI: Omnigraphics, 2009.

Ballard, Carol. *Heart and Blood: Injury, Illness, and Health* (Body Focus). 2nd ed. Chicago, IL: Heinemann Library, 2009.

Bijlefeld, Marjolijn, and Sharon K. Zoumbaris. *Food and You: A Guide to Healthy Habits for Teens*. Westport, CT: Greenwood Press, 2001.

Bjorklund, Ruth. *Circulatory System* (The Amazing Human Body). New York, NY: Marshall Cavendish Benchmark, 2009.

Corcoran, Mary K., and Jef Czekaj. *The Circulatory Story*. Watertown, MA: Charlesbridge, 2010.

Englehart, Deirdre. *Health, Hygiene, and Nutrition, Grades 5-6*. Grand Rapids, MI: Instructional Fair, 2005.

Graimes, Nicola. *Kids' Fun and Healthy Cookbook*. New York, NY: DK, 2007.

Hartman, Eve, and Wendy Meshbesher. *Health and Wellness*. Chicago, IL: Raintree, 2009.

Heller, Marla. *The DASH Diet Action Plan: Proven to Lower Blood Pressure and Cholesterol Without Medication*. Deerfield, IL: Amidon Press, 2007.

Hovius, Christopher. *The Best You Can Be: A Teen's Guide to Fitness and Nutrition* (Science of Health, Youth, and Well-Being). Philadelphia, PA: Mason Crest Publishers, 2005.

Kedge, Joanna, and Joanna Watson. *Fitness* (Teen Issues). Mankato, MN: Raintree Publishers, 2005.

Meek, Janis P. *Nutrition, Food, and Fitness: Student Activity Guide*. Tinley Park, IL: Goodheart-Willcox Co., 2006.

Meeks, Linda Brower, and Philip Heit. *Health and Wellness*. New York, NY: McGraw-Hill/Glencoe, 2005.

Miller, Edward. *The Monster Health Book: A Guide to Eating Healthy, Being Active & Feeling Great for Monsters & Kids!* New York, NY: Holiday House, 2006.

Rockwell, Lizzy. *Good Enough to Eat: A Kid's Guide to Food and Nutrition*. New York, NY: HarperCollins, 2009.

Simon, Seymour. *The Heart: Our Circulatory System*. Rev. ed. New York, NY: Harper-Collins, 2006.

Thorne, Gerard. *Teen Fit for Girls: Your Complete Guide to Fun, Fitness, and Self-Esteem*. Mississauga, ON, Canada: Robert Kennedy Publishing, 2004.

Thorne, Gerard. *Teen Fit for Guys: Your Complete Guide to Fun, Fitness, and Self-Esteem*. Mississauga, ON, Canada: Robert Kennedy Publishing, 2004.

Wallach, Marlene, and Grace Norwich. *My Life: A Guide to Health & Fitness*. New York, NY: Aladdin, 2009.

World Book, Inc. *The Circulatory System* (World Book's Human Body Works). Chicago, IL: World Book, 2007.

American Heart Association. "Blood Pressure." Retrieved October 23, 2009 (http://www.americanheart.org/presenter. jhtml?identifier=4473).

American Heart Association. "What Is High Blood Pressure?" October 19, 2009. Retrieved October 27, 2009 (http://www. americanheart.org/presenter.jhtml?identifier=2152).

Beck, Melinda. "A Salty Tale: Why We Need a Diet Less Rich in Sodium." April 9, 2009. Retrieved October 29, 2009 (http:// online.wsj.com/article/SB124027886933637727.html).

Blood Pressure Updates. "9 Myths About Hypertension." Retrieved October 27, 2009 (http://www.blood-pressure-updates.com/ bp/bp-basics/myths-and-facts/9-top-myths-about-high-blood- pressure-busted.htm).

Carroll, David, and Wahida Karmally. *Controlling High Blood Pressure the Natural Way*. New York, NY: Ballantine Books, 2000.

EHealth MD. "High Blood Pressure." Retrieved October 27, 2009 (http://www.ehealthmd.com/library/highbp/HBP_whatis.html).

EHealth MD. "What Factors Affect Blood Pressure?" Retrieved October 27, 2009 (http://www.ehealthmd.com/library/highbp/ HBP_how.html#factors).

Family Doctor. "High Blood Pressure: Things You Can Do to Help Lower Yours." Retrieved October 23, 2009 (http:// familydoctor.org/online/famdocen/home/common/heartdisease/ risk/092.html).

Mayo Clinic. "Exercise: A Drug-Free Approach to Lowering High Blood Pressure." August 7, 2008. Retrieved October 29, 2009 (http://www.mayoclinic.com/health/high-blood-pressure/HI00024).

Mayo Clinic. "Fitness Programs: 5 Steps to Getting Started." May 19, 2008. Retrieved November 2, 2009 (http://www.mayoclinic. com/health/fitness/HQ00171).

Mayo Clinic. "How Does Caffeine Affect Blood Pressure?" November 14, 2007. Retrieved October 29, 2009 (http://www. mayoclinic.com/health/blood-pressure/AN00792).

Mayo Clinic. "Sodium: Are You Getting Too Much?" Retrieved October 28, 2009 (http://www.mayoclinic.com/health/sodium/ NU00284).

Mayo Clinic. "Stress and High Blood Pressure: What's the Connection?" August 7, 2008. Retrieved November 1, 2009 (http://www.mayoclinic.com/health/stress-and-high-blood-pressure/HI00092).

New York Daily News. "Not Getting Enough Sleep Leads to High Blood Pressure, Study Finds." June 9, 2009. Retrieved October 29, 2009 (http://www.nydailynews.com/lifestyle/health/ 2009/06/09/2009-06-09_not_getting_enough_sleep_leads_to_ high_blood_pressure_study_finds.html).

Sheps, Sheldon G. *Mayo Clinic on High Blood Pressure*. Rochester, MN: Mayo Clinic, 2002.

Web MD. "Causes of High Blood Pressure." Retrieved October 27, 2009 (http://www.webmd.com/hypertension-high-blood-pressure/ guide/blood-pressure-causes).

Web MD. "High Blood Pressure and Smoking." Retrieved October 27, 2009 (http://www.webmd.com/hypertension-high-blood-pressure/ guide/kicking-habit).

Web MD. "Questions to Ask a Doctor About High Blood Pressure." Retrieved October 23, 2009 (http://www.webmd.com/

hypertension-high-blood-pressure/guide/questions-ask-doctor-hypertension).

Web MD. "Stress and High Blood Pressure." Retrieved October 31, 2009 (http://www.webmd.com/hypertension-high-blood-pressure/guide/hypertension-easing-stress).

Web MD. "13 Healthy Habits to Improve Life." Retrieved October 20, 2009 (http://www.webmd.com/balance/features/13-healthy-habits-to-improve-your-life?page=4).

Web MD. "Understanding Low Blood Pressure: The Basics." Retrieved October 28, 2009 (http://www.webmd.com/heart/understanding-low-blood-pressure-basics).

Zeratsky, Katherine. "Why Do Processed Foods Contain So Much Sodium?" September 5, 2008. Retrieved October 29, 2009 (http://www.mayoclinic.com/health/food-and-nutrition/AN00350).

INDEX

About the Author

Laura La Bella is a writer and editor living in Rochester, New York. Among her books, La Bella has profiled actress and activist Angelina Jolie in *Celebrity Activists: Angelina Jolie: Goodwill Ambassador to the UN*; reported on the declining availability of the world's fresh water supply in *Not Enough to Drink: Pollution, Drought, and Tainted Water Supplies*; and has examined the food industry in *Safety and the Food Supply*.

Photo Credits

Cover © www.istockphoto.com/Oscar Gutierrez; p. 5 © www.istockphoto.com/Lisa F. Young; p. 8 © www.istockphoto.com/Sebastian Kaulitzki; p. 9 © www.istockphoto.com/Alexander Katina; pp. 12–13 © www.istockphoto.com; p. 15 © www.istockphoto.com/Elena Elisseeva; p. 17 © Shutterstock; p. 21 © www.istockphoto.com/Joe Biafore; pp. 22–23 © www.istockphoto.com/James McQuillan; p. 26 © www.istockphoto.com/Alex Broca; p. 32 © www.istockphoto.com/Carmen Martinez Banus; p. 34 © www.istockphoto.com/Alberto L. Pomares G.; p. 35 © www.istockphoto.com/Jim Kolaczko; pp. 38–39 © www.istockphoto.com; p. 45 © www.istockphoto.com/Krzysztof Kwiatkowski; p. 46 Wayne Wilson/Getty Images; p. 49 © Bill Aron/Photo Edit; p. 51 © www.istockphoto.com.

Designer: Nicole Russo; Editor: Andrea Sclarow; Photo Researcher: Marty Levick